INTIMATE GUARDIAN

R.K. CARY

SISTERS ROMANCE

CONTENTS

CHAPTER 1

The apple was the start of it. The damned apple. It stared at her, watching her become more upset with each second that passed. She felt the rind in her teeth and tasted the tartness in her mouth, but for the life of her, she couldn't remember getting it from the kitchen or taking a bite from it. It wasn't just the apple, of course, it was the other things, the erotic dreams that seemed so real, the shadowy stranger whose touch was igniting, the constant mental distraction that made focusing impossible. Was this what it felt like to lose your mind?

Emma Oliver had feared this day would come, well, for as long as she could remember. She had just celebrated her twenty-eighth birthday, the same age her mother had been when the schizophrenia hit her and destroyed her life. Was this what it was like for her mother? Emma wished she were still alive, so she could ask her. She wished her mother had been a part of her life and hadn't lost her mind and disappeared when Emma was a small child. She and her father assumed her mother to be long dead. An exhaustive search never located her.

Emma's hand shook as she grabbed hold of her laptop. Work was the last thing she wanted to do. She considered searching through more articles on-line to try to self-diagnose her declining mental state. What she really wanted to do was go back to sleep and feel the passionate kisses and the warm caresses from the intimate intruder in her dreams. She wanted to see his face. He was always cloaked in the shadows. She felt as though she knew him, though. There was a familiarity, a comfort she felt when he was near. She rubbed her eyes and laid her head back against the couch cushion. She stared at the ceiling and breathed out heavily.

***

Mist hung in the air, water droplets that didn't moisten her. A fog blanketed the area. The space was white and airy, tranquil and safe. The temperature was perfect, not too hot and not too cold. It felt ethereal and everything moved in slow motion. She wore a long white gown. It was strappy, sexy, shear. A slight breeze rustled the fabric and her shoulder-length dark hair.

She felt his presence. He was near. She closed her eyes, which was the only way he would engage with her. She felt his touch on her face, his fingers softly drawing her lips to his. She felt his breath over her lips. His were nearing.

Her body yearned for him, for his touch, his closeness. Every nerve ending bristled, crying out for him to warm her skin with his fingers, his mouth, his...yes. To be kissed by him, caressed by him, filled by him. The sensations were overwhelming, exhilarating, orgasmic.

She felt his weight on her body, his breath on her neck, the gentle pressure on the inside of her thighs as her knees were spread. She gasped out as he made contact with her most intimate places.

"Yes," she moaned breathlessly.

The tinkling of chimes invaded her pleasure. The fog lifted. A chill and blackness crept in. She opened her eyes and the light streaming through the windows assaulted her eyes. She was in her apartment. The tinkling repeated. She reached around, feeling for her cell phone. Her hand found it and grabbed it, Talia.

"Fuck," Emma cursed aloud and then swiped to answer. "Yeah," she grunted.

"The WebEx started five minutes ago! I can't cover for you much longer. Where the hell are you?"

"Fuck," she repeated as she grabbed her laptop and rushed to login.

"What's going on with you?" Talia demanded. "Are you trying to get fired?"

"No, I'm just not feeling well today," Emma said. Yes, it was lame. It was the excuse she had used for weeks now.

"Then you need to get your ass to the doctor. Mitch isn't going to buy that much longer," Talia snorted. "Okay, good, I see you're on."

"Yeah, I'm in. I'll talk to you later. And thanks," Emma said before disconnecting the call.

She struggled through the meeting and the rest of her workday. Talia was right. Their boss, Mitch, would not put up with her much longer. Working from home was a luxury. He would surely pull the permission soon, given her poor performance recently.

The darkness of night invaded her tiny apartment, and she still had not moved from the couch, nor did she turn any lights on. Only the glow from her laptop lit the room. At least she was still awake. She gave herself props for that.

The tinkling chimed, her phone screen coming to life. Talia, again. "Hello," she greeted with no enthusiasm.

"Are you home?" Her friend asked.

"Yeah, why?"

"Why is your place dark?" Talia asked.

Emma pulled herself up and gazed out the window. Down three flights at street level, beneath a dim streetlight, stood Talia, gazing up at her. "Come on up," Emma invited.

She turned a light on and glanced around at the clutter and mess strewn about the small kitchen and living room area, all of one hundred square feet. It was too late to make any of it presentable. She stared at her own reflection in the mirror beside the door. That was another thing there was no time to make presentable.

When had she showered last? Hell, when had she brushed her hair last, for that matter? She had dark bags under her brown eyes. She pulled her hair into a ponytail, securing it with one of the four elastic covered rubber bands on her wrist. She sniffed the fingers of her right hand. She smelled herself on them, the scent the intruder in her dreams told her he loved as his mouth pleasured her with intimate kisses as no man ever had. Too late to go wash her hands because two harsh raps hit her door. Talia.

She opened it and stepped aside, letting the perky blond in. She gazed at her friend, bracing herself. Talia's bright blue eyes swept the room and over Emma. She sighed and brought the takeout bag that had incredible aromas leaking from it over to the little kitchen table Emma hadn't eaten at since probably the last time Talia had been over. There were two spaces open, the two other chairs and the tabletop in front of them were littered with crap.

Emma glanced at her dark blue sweatshirt. She was probably wearing this same shirt the last time Talia had been over. She knew she hadn't done laundry in weeks. She watched Talia unpacked the bag. Chinese, her favorite.

Emma retrieved plastic silverware and two paper plates from the cabinet. All her dishes and cutlery were dirty and stacked in the sink and the counter beside it. She then grabbed two water bottles from the refrigerator. At least she had water in a clean container to offer.

"If I wasn't incredibly worried about you, I would yell at you right now," Talia said, her Russian accent heavy and lacing every word tonight. That tended to happen when Talia was excited or pissed.

Talia just stared at her, waiting for her to say something, anything. The problem was, Emma didn't know what to say. She knew her behavior was not normal. She was barely functioning. Today's meeting that she nearly missed was not the first. She didn't expect to have a job much longer at this rate. How could she explain any of this to Talia? She felt terrible.

Talia had been a great friend and the fact that she was here, and had brought food, proved that.

"You look like hell," Talia finally said, dishing out entrees from the three cartons she brought.

Emma nodded her agreement.

"After we eat, you're going to shower and then you and I will clean this place up. I'm staying over, and I made you an appointment for you with a doctor tomorrow. I'm bringing you to that appointment," Talia said.

Tears filled Emma's eyes. "I'm really afraid."

Talia reached across the table and took her hand. "I know you are, and I'm here for you. If it is the schizophrenia, you need to know and get on some meds. It doesn't have to mean the end of your life or independence. There are better drugs available now than when your mother took them." Talia paused, watching Emma. "Besides, it can't be that bad yet. I don't see tinfoil everywhere." Talia smiled.

Emma laughed. "I don't even remember the last time I went to the store. I don't have any. That's probably the only reason there isn't."

Talia laughed, too. The grocery store, that was something else they would have to go do tomorrow.

CHAPTER 2

Emma did feel better, cleaning herself and her apartment up. That short-lived feeling left her as soon as Talia led her through the doorway to the Behavioral Health Clinic at nine the next morning. Talia filled her patient forms out while sitting beside her. Emma felt numb. Her eyes remained on the large clock on the wall. It seemed like they had waited for hours, but the large hand on the clock had only spanned twenty minutes before she was called back. Talia went with her.

They were ushered into an office with a desk and visitor's chairs, as well as a couch. The room was decorated in shades of blues and greens, subdued and calming hues. A few minutes later, a petite older woman entered, dressed in a soft pink dress, wearing four-inch heels. Her blondish-gray hair was swept up in a chignon, framing a face that boasted high cheekbones and deep-set green eyes.

Hello Emma, "I'm Doctor Kimberly Raymond," she greeted, her hand outstretched towards Emma.

Emma forced a smile and shook her hand. *How did she know I was Emma and not Talia? Oh, that's right; the front desk took my ID. She'd have reviewed my file before entering.* "Hello," she forced herself to say.

"And you must be her friend," Dr. Raymond said to Talia.

"Yes, I'm Talia Sokolov and I made the appointment for Emma. Something is really wrong with her. Her behavior and performance at work has rapidly declined over the past few weeks."

"Month," Emma corrected her. "It's been at least a month."

Dr. Raymond nodded. She asked Talia some questions to get a picture of what she saw happening. Emma sat awkwardly while Talia detailed out her decline. She reported it quite well, actually. All she was missing was the sexual nature of the shadowy man who had invaded her dreams. Of course, Talia knew nothing about him. Then Talia was sent out of the room by Doctor Raymond.

Dr. Raymond took a seat beside her on the couch. The shrink's couch, Emma wondered, shouldn't she be lying down? She chuckled to herself at that thought. Dr. Raymond regarded her with a pleasant expression.

"Would you say your friend captured your behavior well?"

"Yep, she nailed it."

"You're having problems sleeping?" She asked.

"No, I sleep all the time. Can't stay awake, actually," Emma answered.

"Would you describe yourself as being stressed or anxious?"

"I am now," Emma said with a laugh.

The doctor's lips tugged upward. "Your mother had schizophrenia," she stated it as a fact. Emma nodded. "That does not mean that you will be afflicted with it as well."

"The odds are high, though," Emma said.

"Emma, I heard your friend's version of how you're acting. Now I want to hear from you why your behavior has changed. Why are you here?" Dr. Raymond asked.

"I'm losing my mind," Emma replied softly. "That's really the only explanation for what is happening to me."

"And what is happening to you?" Kimberly Raymond pressed.

Emma's eyes met hers. Then her gaze darted away. "I'm hearing voices and this man is haunting my dreams. He's familiar, and he says he's always been with me."

"Voices? When you're awake or asleep?"

"I don't really know; the two states overlap."

This got Dr. Raymond's attention. "And what do these voices say to you?"

Emma paused, deep in thought. It was always the same, the mist, the fog, the sexual desire, the familiar stranger. He did always talk to her. "He says he's always been with me, watching over me and protecting me. He says one day he will come for me, and we'll be together." Emma paused as her eyes met Dr. Raymond's.

"Have you ever asked him how he protects you?"

"I've never spoken to him."

"Why not?"

Emma laughed. Good question. Why hadn't she? "It just never occurred to me to engage him in conversation," she admitted.

"I think you should next time. Keep a pad of paper and pen by you and write any interactions with this man. Make sure it is beside your bed. Write what he says and exactly what happens as soon as you wake."

Emma nodded. Yes, she'd do that. She'd be brave and talk to this intruder.

The doctor went through a long assessment survey with her, asking her question after question. Emma answered all questions honestly. She figured she might as well make the most of this appointment. She wasn't having much luck with self-diagnosing herself. She hoped the doctor could. Maybe Talia was right. Maybe it wasn't as bad as she feared.

"Emma, I'm going to order a full battery of blood work to rule anything else out, but I don't think you need to obsess that you are becoming schizophrenic. I'm not seeing anything that will lead me in that direction."

The doctor handed over two prescriptions. The first was for the blood work, the second was for Xanax. "It's a light antianxiety medication. I want you to take it upon waking, midday, and then again before bed. Try to keep to a routine, bathing, cleaning up after yourself and eating normal meals at normal times."

Emma nodded she would. The blood draw to check her blood for everything possible would be done immediately in the lab portion of the clinic. She made three more appointments with the doctor before she left. Talia escorted her to the pharmacy and then watched Emma take her first pill, to be sure she took it. Then they went to the grocery store. Talia helped her put the groceries away at her apartment.

"Okay, I'll be back on Monday to bring you to your doctor's appointment," Talia said.

Emma knew she'd check the apartment out as well to see if she was keeping it picked up. Talia would probably count her pills as well to see if she was taking the meds. Talia could be tenacious like that. Emma smiled as she watched her blond head retreat down the long hallway. She closed and locked the door. She stripped her clothes off and went right to her bed. Might as well make it easier for her dream man.

CHAPTER 3

Emma melted into her bed. The fresh scent of the detergent and fabric softener on the recently washed sheets caressed her nose. It was like she was lying in a flower garden. She was warm, relaxed, and comfortable. She floated effortlessly, enjoying the calm sensations washing through her. It didn't take long for the fog to roll in.

***

Light wisps floated in first, followed by a solid wall that blocked everything else out. She felt his presence. He was near. She saw his shadow at the edge of the cloudy blanket over the horizon where spires and steeples suddenly sprung up carving holes in the fluff. That was new. Xanax induced?

He lightly ran his fingers over her face, so she'd close her eyes. He liked her eyes to be closed. His fingers traced her jawbone from her ear to her chin and they then drew a line down her neck. She gasped as the light touch slowly ran straight down her chest, down her abdomen, over her pelvis, and to the apex of her legs. She unconsciously spread her legs.

As his fingers penetrated her, she felt his lips on her right nipple, always the right first. Now she moaned. She remembered she was to engage him. It took great effort to open her eyes. The top of his dark head was so close, black hair falling long over his face, pooling on her chest. A bright light behind him cast his face in a shadow. He moved his mouth to the left nipple as his fingers curled and stroked her g-spot with a rhythm that nearly sent her over the edge. She moaned louder, unable to concentrate on anything other than the incredible sensations he brought her.

"Come for me," his breathy, deep voice commanded.

"Why do you want me to come?" she asked.

He froze for a moment, shocked she had spoken. He didn't answer. When he returned to his ministrations, it was with a renewed focus, an all-out assault that had her screaming her pleasure in seconds. As she recovered from a shattering release, he slid his mouth to her mound and attacked her clit with equal energy.

"Oh my God, that feels amazing," she said aloud.

She reached her hands to him and stroked over his soft hair. As always, he took hold of her hands and drew them away from him, placing them on the bed beside her legs. He never let her touch him for longer than a second. Usually she would keep them where he put them, an unspoken rule. Not this time. When his hand caressed over her abdomen and ran up to her breasts, she returned her hand to him, grasping his muscled arms and feeling his shoulders.

He gently removed her hands and returned them to the bed. He tucked them beneath her bottom, spread her legs wider and he added fingers plunging into her core to the intense kisses his mouth was giving her intimate lips. She bucked as the sensation pushed her to the edge, panting turned into whimpers that turned into screams. She was blinded by bright lights behind her closed eyes. All the while, his warm mouth made love to her and his fingers brought pleasure to her deepest regions.

She was still breathless when she felt his weight upon her, his knees on the insides of her thighs, his head pressing against her entrance. Breaking another unspoken rule, she opened her eyes and gazed into the face of her lover, into his dark eyes, his chiseled cheekbones, and strong jaw that had a shadow of growth on it. She'd always felt the stubble. This was the first time she had opened her eyes to see his face. He was beautiful, masculine, familiar.

His eyes flashed something she couldn't read before his hand gently ran over her eyes, his silent instruction to keep them closed.

"Why can't I see you, know who you are?" she asked.

He breathed out a strangled moan as he pressed into her, to which she groaned out her pleasured response. His cheek was beside hers, held barely against it, his breath on her ear. She heard his pleasured sighs as he pumped into her, an agonizingly slow rhythm. His breaths came quicker, laced with more pleasure as he plunged deeper and faster. She tingled deep inside; her walls gripped him. Her third orgasm was on the horizon.

She reached her arms around him and held his lower back with one hand, the back of his shoulder with the other. She groped where her hands lay. At the contact, another no-no in their carnal act, he roared out louder than he ever had, and he plunged in deeply, none too gently, which he had always been with her. He swelled to an incredible girth, and she felt filled in a way she had never felt with anyone before, including him. She felt the orgasm rush over her, a different sensation than she normally experienced. At the feel of her core milking his shaft, his cries became strangled. He sounded tortured. His entire body quaked, and she felt his seed fill her, a warm fluid she knew was real.

He held her tightly, his face buried in her neck. "You disobeyed me," he said softly.

"How, by speaking to you and touching you?"

Her hands still gripped him. She caressed over his warm, solid body. He sure felt real.

"In all things, there is a time. It is not yet our time."

"When will it be?"

"You will know when. Until then, you must obey."

"Or what? You won't return?" she demanded. She still felt his cock inside her. It throbbed. A thought came to her. "I doubt that. You crave this as much as I do, maybe more. You are the one who comes to me."

"You summon me," he corrected her. "I do not come to you."

"So, I'm the one who controls this?" she asked. She felt a new sense of power.

"You must obey. The time has not yet come," he repeated.

***

A chill swept over her; the fog receded. She opened her eyes to discover the bedcovers pushed from her. She was alone in her bedroom. The images and sensations were fresh in her thoughts. She grabbed the pad of paper and pen and she furiously detailed out the encounter.

Emma did her best to keep the house clean over the weekend. She opted to continue to use disposable plates and cutlery. She didn't want to risk that the sink would become overloaded with dirty dishes again, as she didn't trust herself to take care of them.

After rereading her notes on the several sexual encounters she'd had with the intruder over the two days since her doctor's appointment, she became convinced he was real. Her mind could not have produced the detail that continued to evolve in the 'dreams'. Her new online searches focused on alternate realities and dimensions, visitors from outer space, and even time travel.

What she found was startling. There were accounts from others with similar visitations, both men and women experiencing them. Following link after link brought her to a forum of posts. No one used real names, but what she would describe as stripper names. She signed up as Sex Dreamer and chose a curvaceous female cartoon avatar to represent her.

Then she got busy reading the posts, shocked how similar they were to each other and to her experiences. Only a few people sought professional help, most not believing it was anything medical or mental causing the visitations. Those who did, came back with mixed experiences. One man, with heavy medication, rid himself of what he called the delusions. Several others discontinued treatment citing that it didn't help, nothing medical was found to be wrong.

She posted replies to a few of the recent threads. There was one woman, Unicorn Chaser, that had been having the visitations for eight years, since she'd turned twenty-one. Emma couldn't even think how she would go on like this for even another month, let alone eight years. If this went on another month, she doubted she'd have a job, which meant shortly thereafter, she wouldn't have a place to live.

Peace, darkness, the wisps of fog rolling in. She felt his presence. The spires with glowing blue lights poked from the bottom of the fog. She was high in the sky, a new realization. Before her, a brass railing, chest high. She laid her hand on it. It was cool to the touch.

From behind her, a hand laid to her shoulder, gently gripping her. "Come back to bed, my love," the familiar deep voice of her lover said.

She turned to face him and found they stood on a balcony. Behind him was a building, an oddly familiar building in an ultra-modern design. Even the opening into it was unlike any door she'd entered.

She took his hand, and he led her within, into a space with soft lighting radiating up the four walls in shades of blue. A large bed lay in the middle of the room. That was all that was there. Just one step in and he effortlessly lifted her from her feet, cradling her in his muscular, strong arms. He carried her to the bed and laid her on her back in the middle of it.

She gazed into his dark eyes. He no longer attempted to stop her from viewing him. As he reclined above her, he stroked his knuckles over her cheek. Even though the lighting was low in the room, she got a good look at him. His face was masculine, attractive. He had clear skin, slightly bronzed, with a chiseled, perfect bone structure. His hair was black, thick, and flowed below his shoulders. It was shiny, and she knew it was soft.

He raised her chin with his cupped hand and she watched with great desire as his lips neared hers. The kiss was soft, passionate and instantly she became wet. His fingers caressed with soft touches down her neck and over her right breast, teasing her already erect nipple. Everywhere he stroked, she tingled, feeding the intense sexual desire that increased with every touch.

Her hands kneaded his shoulders and then traveled up his neck, felt over his face, and then speared into his soft locks. After she enjoyed the sensation long enough, she allowed her hands to feel over his back. Her fingers memorized every inch of him, every inch of his muscled, warm, naked body.

She was beyond ready when he pulled his lips from hers and they trailed kisses everywhere over her awaiting flesh. Soft, wet kisses left trails of goosebumps. With the untying of the satin ribbon that held the strappy, sexy, sheer negligee together over her breasts, he exposed her to himself and sighed in contentment. He never took it completely from her, though. His mouth took her right breast while his hand caressed over her left nipple.

He had her nearly on the edge of an orgasm from just the attention he showed her breasts. When he left a trail of wet kisses down her abdomen, she knew what he would do next to her anxious body. The moisture between her legs increased with just the anticipation of his mouth giving her intimate parts, the intense kisses he always lavished on her.

He pressed a kiss to her clit, which garnered a loud and needy sigh from her. She heard a low chuckle in return from him. Then he licked her with a hard tongue, down her clit and deep inside her. Her hands fisted the sheets and her back arched off them. He blew a hot breath over her exposed, very engorged clit, which made her back arch higher from the mattress. The insides of her thighs quivered.

"Please," she whimpered. "I'm so close."

He blew two more breaths while his hands firmly massaged her inner thighs, brushing her parts as they kneaded her near her apex. Then she felt a single finger trace over her from her throbbing clit, over her wet and open vagina, down further, and over the skin of her anus, where he'd never touched her before. He didn't penetrate her anywhere. She gasped out the entire few minutes that his finger made its journey.

Then as he cupped each of her butt cheeks in a hand, lifting them slightly into the air to splay her more open to him, he lowered his head to her and feasted on her clit, her drenched vagina, and his tongue even ventured to her quivering anus, a sensation so intense she screamed out pure sexual satisfaction laced with a need for complete fulfillment.

Transferring her bottom into one hand, he devoured her clit while his fingers plunged into her awaiting hole, his fingers penetrating her to her core. He twisted them and plunged them in and out of her. Her pleasure-filled moans and screams filled the room, culminating in a grunt so tortured and deep she didn't recognize it as a sound she was capable of producing. It, of course, accompanied a tightening and straining of her body as the most intense orgasm she ever experienced ripped through her body, which quaked with the tremors of the incredible release.

Then, as she expected, he gave her several slow, passionate open-mouth kisses to her super-sensitive clit. He ran his tongue over her and then his mouth captured her throbbing clit and he sucked on it, making her orgasm again. She was still trembling when his tongue teased it more, building her up towards another release. She moaned and her body continued to quake as though she was having a seizure. Right when she was on the edge, he got in position, pressing his large, long member to her drenched opening.

He plunged in with a gasp and a loud moan, instantly filling her. She moaned in response. His face was nestled in her neck. She felt his hot breaths. "I'm going to make love to you like I never have. Do you give yourself to me and only me?"

This was the first time he had asked her a direct question or ask for a commitment. "Yes, I am yours," she proclaimed.

"You were created for me and me alone. Our time to remain together is nearing. Soon, we will never be parted," he said.

That was the last she comprehended. He maneuvered himself so that her pelvis raised from the bed, his knees slipping in beneath her butt. Her legs dropped open and away from his legs, giving him deeper access, which brought a pleasure on the edge of pain groan from her. He plunged in and out with speed, gaining depth. Her brain was overloaded with the sensation. A part of her wanted to scream in agony, the other part wanted to beg him to never stop, the pleasure overwhelming.

The orgasm that overtook her was powerful, consuming. She was barely aware of his own orgasm and screams that accompanied it. He was pressed so deeply inside her, it was a fullness she'd never experienced. He lowered her butt to the bed, keeping himself pressed deep inside her. His face came to rest beside hers and his hands held her with tender caresses where they touched.

She held him with trust and affection, and complete sexual satisfaction. She felt herself drift, sleep approaching. "Promise you'll be here when I wake," she begged.

"I will. Now sleep, my love."

CHAPTER 4

When Emma woke, it was to the tinkling of chimes. Her eyes viewed the familiar walls of her bedroom. She lay on her bed, wrapped in her bedding, naked. He wasn't there. Sadness and anger filled her. He'd promised. The chimes sounded again, her phone which sat on her bedside table.

"Hello," she barked into it.

"Good morning to you, too," Talia replied. "I'll be over in thirty minutes to pick you up for your doctor's appointment."

Emma groaned. She didn't want to go, didn't believe any longer this was mental or medical. "Right, I'll be ready. If you want, call when you're here and I'll come down so you don't have to mess with finding a parking spot." Plus, she didn't want Talia to come check on her place.

"Sounds good. See you soon."

She sat the phone back on the bedside table and noticed the pad of paper. No, she wouldn't record this latest 'dream'. She was done doing that. She got up, took a quick shower, threw her hair back into a ponytail and dressed in clean clothes. Thirty minutes later, when Talia called, she was ready.

She slid into the passenger seat of Talia's old Ford Fiesta. "Thanks for picking me up."

"You look better rested today."

"I went to bed early and slept great. I guess this Xanax is helping," Emma said. She credited it for bringing out greater detail in her dreams.

"Good," Talia said as she pulled away from the curb.

"Why are we off work again today?" Emma asked.

"Today is Martin Luther King Day," Talia said. "But brace yourself. I already looked at the calendar for tomorrow. We have meeting after meeting. Something is up. I'm not sure what, but I'm worried."

If Talia was worried, that worried Emma. Talia didn't worry about much. "Why do you think that?"

"Some of the meeting topics are team realignments, product changes, and recalls."

A dread settled in Emma's stomach. She hadn't checked her calendar for the next day. She wasn't sure if she had all the meeting invitations that Talia had. She suddenly worried she may lose her job and that would cause team realignments. Even if she kept her job but was moved to a different team than Talia was on, that would bring sudden death to her career. Talia really had been covering her ass and keeping her on track, somewhat, for the past month. She'd check her laptop as soon as she got home.

They arrived at the clinic and were only seated in the waiting room a few minutes before Emma was called back to Dr. Raymond's office. Talia remained in the waiting room.

Dr. Raymond was within her office. "Hi Emma, how are you today?"

Emma closed the door. "I think better. I think the Xanax is helping. I'm sleeping better and feel less anxiety, of course I haven't had work the past few days, so I'm not worrying about that."

"And the dreams?"

Emma took a seat on the couch. Dr. Raymond sat at her desk and picked up a tablet from the desktop, holding it on her lap.

"Still intense." She wouldn't tell the doctor she no longer believed them to be just dreams, but rather was sure they were visitations. "But it's different now. They no longer frighten me."

"What is different about them?"

"I don't know. Maybe the Xanax, or maybe since I've told someone about them it's different."

"Did you speak to this man in your dreams?"

"Yes, we're having conversations now. At first he told me it wasn't time for us to speak yet, but I kept asking him things and he replied."

"What's his name?" Dr. Raymond asked.

Emma smiled and chuckled a short burst. "I don't know. I haven't asked him."

Dr. Raymond smiled. "Maybe that should be your next question to him. Don't you want to know the name of this intruder?"

Emma nodded.

"What else does he say?"

"That I was made for him, or did he say created? I don't recall." She wouldn't tell the doctor of his demand that she declare he was her one and only, nor would she tell her the greater detail that was emerging from each dream.

"Did that frighten you?"

"No, it was comforting. He and the dreams never really frightened me in themselves, it was the thought that I was losing my mind that frightened me."

"Do you still believe you are losing your mind?" Dr. Raymond asked.

"You tell me," Emma said with a forced smile.

"Well," she said, typing into her tablet and viewing the results. "All your bloodwork came back completely normal. You seem calmer today, so I'm going to say the Xanax is working. You will be back to work tomorrow. Let's see how your focus on work is for the rest of the week. That will be a true indication of how things are progressing. And if you continue to bathe, eat, and keep your apartment clean, that too will tell us a lot."

Emma nodded. "I am worried about my job. I've missed a lot of deadlines, been late to meetings, and

I know the quality of my work took a nose-dive over the last month."

"Most employers will give warnings. If you receive one you can choose to disclose that you are seeing a doctor. You do not need to disclose the nature of the illness."

Emma felt weird about that. She doubted she would go that route. "We'll see."

Dr. Raymond gave her a smile. "I'd say continue taking the Xanax. If you find it difficult to remain focused, make yourself a daily checklist of to-do items such as showering, eating, cleaning up the kitchen, and so forth. Keep a detailed to-do list for work so you miss no more meetings or deadlines. Live by those lists."

Emma nodded, though she knew it wouldn't help. You couldn't read to-do lists if you were asleep and she couldn't wait to get home and go back to sleep. She had several questions she wanted to ask her dream lover. His name, something so basic. Why hadn't she thought to ask him his name?

"Our time is about up," Dr. Raymond said. "Do you have any other questions for me?"

"No, I'm good," Emma answered. "I'll do everything you suggested and let you know how it's going at our next appointment. I really feel better and really do believe that I am not losing my mind now."

Dr. Raymond smiled. "Very good." She came to her feet. "Keep taking the Xanax and recording the contents of the dreams. Bring your notebook next time and we'll analyze the dreams together."

Emma came to her feet as well. "Okay, I will." Though she knew she had no intention of writing any more in the notebook or discussing it with the doctor.

When she returned to the waiting room, Talia came to her feet. They exited and Talia waited until they were within the private confines of her car to ask anything. "How'd it go?"

"The blood tests all came back normal. I do feel a lot better. I don't know if it is just the Xanax masking how I really feel, but I don't feel anxious and I'm not worrying that I'm losing my mind any longer."

"That's great!"

"I think just having a professional to talk to has really helped, not that you haven't been great."

Talia chuckled. "Yes, I was feeling like chopped liver, not that it's a bad thing, chopped liver that is. I like a good spread on water crackers, served with caviar."

"And a glass of champagne," Emma added.

"While accompanying a tall, handsome, rich man to an elegant affair," Talia said with a laugh.

"You and me both," Emma joked.

"In my dreams," Talia admitted.

Emma smiled. She'd take her mystery man in bed in her dreams. She didn't need elegant affairs filling her dreams.

As Emma expected, Talia insisted on coming up to her apartment with her when they got back to it.

"See, no tinfoil anywhere," Emma said jokingly.

"And it's cleaned up. Not even any dishes in the sink."

Emma wrapped her arms around Talia. "Thank you for everything, for being such a good friend that you'd come over here, stay, and take me to the doctor."

"You're my best friend, you know that, right?" Talia said. She still looked concerned.

"You're mine too." Emma hugged her more tightly.

After Talia left, Emma went straight to bed. She had questions for her mystery man. She stripped down and then crawled beneath her covers. She relaxed into her pillow and invited sleep.

It didn't take long for the darkness to give way to fog, this time it was a solid wall of it. She could barely see the brass handrail in front of her, which her hands grasped.

"Come back to bed, my love," the deep voice of her lover called from behind her.

She turned and saw his shadowy figure looming in the open doorway. Wisps of fog separated them. He held a hand out to her. She crossed the patio, her bare feet feeling the cool and textured floor beneath. Taking his hand, she stepped through the threshold, the floor warm and smooth. The walls illuminated that blue light, soft and low.

The bed loomed in the middle of the room, but this time she noticed its shape, round, and the bedcoverings, a light blue made from satin or silk, she wasn't sure which. He pulled the string on his black pants, and they dropped to the floor. Her eyes became transfixed on his cock, hanging long. It wasn't quite erect, but it wasn't flaccid either. It was in an in between state.

He untied the ribbon, holding her shear gown together. This time, he pushed it from her shoulders. It pooled at her feet. Her eyes met his. They had a different quality to them, they sparkled with life in a way they hadn't before.

"What's your name? May I know it?"

"Sabian," his deep voice said.

"You said I'd be with you when I woke."

"Your phone called you back to your realm. The tinkling of the chimes follows you. You need to silence it to remain here. It is not time for you to join me yet, not time for you to cut all ties to your ambit, soon, my love."

"I don't understand what that means," she confessed.

He cupped her face in his hands. "It will be clear to you when the time is upon you." Then he leaned in and kissed her.

His kisses silenced the thoughts and questions that ran through her mind. She melted into him, appreciating his strong, warm body pressed to hers.

Her hands caressed over him, stroked his soft hair, his muscled back, his firm butt cheeks.

When Emma woke, she immediately looked up the word ambit. She didn't know what it meant. Per Myriam-Webster, the definition of ambit was 1: circuit, compass. 2: the bounds or limits of a place or district. 3: a sphere of action, expression, or influence: scope. Then she logged into the forum she'd joined. She made a new post, discussing the word ambit and asking others of this term had been used by their intimate intruders.

She looked back over the past posts she had made, questions she had posed to others who'd made posts. Very few had been answered. Upon a more detailed inspection and analysis, she found most people posted for a few months and then there was nothing more. A dread settled over her. Where had they gone?

She went back to the post with Unicorn Chaser, the woman who had been having visitations for eight years. She initiated a private message. "I need to actually speak with you about something I've noticed in this forum. Please trust me. This is important," she wrote. Then she provided her phone number. "Please call me."

Then she hit send. The site showed that Unicorn Chaser was active on the site. Hopefully she'd get the message and call her soon. Two hours later, still sitting with her laptop on and logged into the forum, and with her phone in her hand, Emma accepted that Unicorn Chaser was probably not going to call. She was disappointed. She was at a loss what to do next. She laid her head back against the couch and closed her eyes.

The air was scented with something citrusy. It was crisp and energizing. The fogbank was solid at first but dissolved into wisps that revealed the spires and the tops of the tall buildings before her. The nearest spire was gold-topped and had a flashing green light at its tip.

She felt her lover's presence. He was within their room waiting for her. She was near the door, not along the railing of the balcony this time. With one step, she was within. The glow of the lighting up the walls was more vibrant. She could see his still form laying in the center of the bed. She untied her own gown as she approached, dropping it to the floor when she reached him.

She crawled atop him and gazed into his eyes, which were lit with a fire that entranced her. "Sabian, you said I was made for you and that you've always been with me."

"Yes, I've always been with you, watching over you and protecting you," he whispered.

"How have you protected me?"

His lips smiled, pleased by her question. "A thought planted in your head, a destination or an idea. Go left not right so you don't cross paths with the serial killer, a person to befriend or one to avoid."

"That's pretty specific, a serial killer?"

"In Atlanta, while you were in college. Had you turned right you would have run into him. He would have seen you and you would have been on his list of prey. I protected you so that you would live to see the day that we would be together."

"When did you start to protect me?"

"The day you were conceived to be mine. I've been with you always," Sabian said. His hands glided along her bare back and over her butt. He undulated beneath her and she felt his hardness against her.

"So, you influenced my thoughts?"

"You didn't always listen. I tried to warn you away from Jimmy Mills when you were fifteen, but you didn't listen."

"Why did you want to warn me away from him?"

"Because I wanted to be your first."

He pressed into her, the sudden invasion jarring. He held her hips and moved her up and down his shaft. Emma knew this was real. There was no way these sensations were in her mind or in her dreams.

She allowed him to use her body, setting the pace. She clenched her muscles to milk his shaft, garnering a deep, guttural moan from inside him. He increased the speed and the depth of his assault on her. She cried out, on the edge of pleasure and pain, not sure which was winning out.

When he came, the sound that escaped him was inhuman. He buried himself so deeply within her it was surely pain. He throbbed, his girth and length unbearable. "You're hurting me," she whimpered.

"You are mine," he said. "You were made to accommodate me. My body fits within yours. Breathe and accept me."

Emma tried to breathe, tried to relax. Her mind reeled. Her dream lover had never hurt her before. Why was he doing this to her? And that sound, that guttural moan, that shriek. It sounded almost demonic. It frightened her.

Her thoughts blanked out when he moved within her again. Before she knew it, she lay on her back. He loomed above her, a larger-than-life figure with fire in his eyes. They glowed red. He pressed in and out of her in a slow rhythm. When he withdrew all the way out of her, she quivered with need. When he surged all the way within, she gasped, the sensation overwhelming.

As he reached his peak, he leaned down, and his lips engulfed the side of her neck. She orgasmed spontaneously when he bit her, a lightning bolt sensation that was as erotic as it was painful. Blinding, white hot fireworks exploded in her head. She drifted, only anchored to this reality by his pulsating shaft deep insider her.

When she woke, she was seated on her couch. Her laptop sat beside her. The message icon within the forum blinked insistently. She immediately went to her mirror. Even though her neck ached where he'd bitten, there was no external mark.

She scrubbed her hand over her face. Confused and shaken, she took another Xanax. Then she returned to the couch and clicked on the message icon. It was from Unicorn Chaser. "I'm sorry, I have no way to call you right now. What have you noticed in the forum?"

Emma summoned her courage to actually detail her thoughts out. Then she typed. "Most of the other posters, they have only been active for a few months. Then they're gone, they post no more. I fear something has happened to them and I now fear for my own safety."

She reread it. Oh, boy, grab the tinfoil and cover the windows with it! She sounded like a paranoid, delusional lunatic. She hit send. Let Unicorn Chaser think she was a whack-job.

Immediately a reply popped in. "I think they were taken to the other realm by their guardians. They are not intruders. They are here to protect us until the day comes that we can be with them."

Emma read that over several times. Sabian had used the word protect. Her words mirrored Sabian's. A chill invaded her. She typed out a new message. "Who are you? Are you one of them?" She sent it without thinking about whether it would piss off Unicorn Chaser.

"I assist those who find me. That is my role until I can be with my guardian." Was the reply.

Emma gasped, now shaking. She stared at the message for a long time.

"He's always been with you. Look back at your life and see him. You need to fully accept him for the time to be upon you to depart with him."

Emma closed out of the forum and shut the lid to her laptop. She sat with her back firmly against the couch. Her hands shook, her heart pounded. She'd never been more frightened in her life. Her eyes darted around her apartment. Was she being watched?

"Get a grip, get a grip, Emma," she said aloud to herself.

On the bookshelf across the room was her
childhood photo album. She felt compelled to look
through it. She brought it back to the couch with
her and flipped through the pages, her eyes scanning
each photo. Her first birthday picture of her in
the highchair with cake mashed all over, he was
there in the shadows in the group behind her. She
would know his form anywhere. Her first day of
kindergarten, beside the pine trees in background, he
stood, watching. Her sixteenth birthday, the party at
the pizza parlor. He was at the edge of her group of
friends, in the shadows, but there. In picture after
picture, he was there, watching, hovering nearby.

She opened the photos folder on her phone. She
flipped through the pictures. In a selfie taken just over
a month earlier, he was there just steps behind her and
Talia. Emma remembered that night. She and Talia
had gone out to a bar for martinis to celebrate the
completion of a big project. That was the night before
the dreams began, before her world began to fall apart.
He was close enough to touch her in that photo. His
face was clear, not masked in shadows. His eyes were

shining, damn-near glowing. They were mesmerizing and she couldn't look away.

She gasped and jumped at the tinkling of her ringtone. Talia. She fought to catch her breath. "Hey," she answered, trying to sound as normal as possible.

"Are you okay?" Talia asked. "I suddenly had an overwhelming feeling that you were in danger."

She pulled the phone away from her ear and stared at it. How did Talia know? She brought the phone back to her ear. "No, everything is fine," she lied.

"You don't sound fine," Talia said. Her voice was accusatory.

"Talia, do you remember when we went out to that martini bar last month?"

"Yes, I didn't drink that much. Of course, I remember."

"Do you still have that picture we took? We each took a selfie of the two of us making a toast. Bring it up, right now, bring it up and look at it. Is there a guy with long black hair right behind us?"

"Hold on," Talia said.

Emma could hear in Talia's voice that she was losing patience. Then she heard a sexy chuckle through the phone. "Oh damn, yeah, he's hot! How didn't I notice him before now?"

"Text me that picture, right now," Emma demanded.

"You have it."

"I need your copy too, please, I can't explain, just send it." Emma knew she sounded desperate, crazy even.

"Okay," Talia agreed.

A few seconds later, Emma was staring at the picture, an identical photo to the one she'd captured. It was real. Sabian was real. He'd been there that night, and many other times throughout her life. She again flipped through the pictures in her photo album. He was the same in them all. He hadn't aged.

"Emma, what are you doing? Are you still there?" Talia's voice came through the phone.

She picked it back up. "I'm sorry, yes, I'm just trying to figure out where I know him from. I noticed him in this picture earlier and I know him. Does he look familiar to you?"

"No, I'd definitely remember him."

"Okay, no worries," Emma said. "I'm fine, but I have to go."

"Call me if you need me," Talia offered, but Emma wasn't listening. Her mind was processing the fact that Sabian had always been near.

CHAPTER 5

This time when Emma laid in her bed, sleep wouldn't come. She tossed and turned and couldn't quiet her thoughts. She took another Xanax, washing it down with a shot of whiskey. Smart no, but effective.

The heavy white wall of clouds moved in. It was so thick she couldn't even see her feet on the flooring, but she felt the textured surface and knew she stood on the balcony. He emerged from the fog; the tendrils clutching at his outline until he broke free from it.

"Do not be afraid of me," his deep voice spoke, echoing through her mind.

"I'm not," she lied.

He moved up to her and stood so close she felt the heat radiate from his body.

"I see it in your eyes, in your features. I feel your fear in your being. I have been with you since the day you were conceived, chosen to be with you, to watch over you," he said. "I feel what you feel. You cannot lie to me."

"What are you?" she asked. "Where is this place?"

"I am your guardian, your lover, the other half of your being. This is my realm and will be yours when you voluntarily make that choice, that conscious choice."

"When will that be?"

"When you are ready. Based on what I feel in you, it sadly is not yet the time."

"You're not human," she whispered, afraid to have him answer, afraid he would confirm what she knew to be fact.

His eyes lit and glowed red. A chill crawled over her skin followed by a cold sweat. His finger lightly traced over her cheek bone.

"I frightened you."

"You hurt me."

"I thought you were prepared, but I was mistaken. I'm sorry I let myself loose when we were last together. I've remained restrained. The advanced intimacy of your hands touching me, of us conversing, of you seeing me for who I am, gave me a false sense that you were ready. There can be no miscalculation when I come to you and ask you to leave your world for mine."

"Leave?" She asked shaking her head. "I can't leave my world."

"You must!" His voice boomed. "And it must be by your choice."

Emma jolted awake and sat straight up in her bed. She was covered in sweat and she shook. Sabian had been larger than life. His eyes glowed red, and a halo of light surrounded him. She wasn't sure what he was. But he definitely wasn't human. It occurred to her that he had not answered the question of what he was.

She got up and turned every light on in her house. It was nighttime, straight up midnight. She grabbed her laptop. First, she logged into her work calendar. Not a single meeting showed for the following day. Talia's calendar was booked. It was what she suspected. She was losing her job. There was no other explanation for her calendar.

She paced around her tiny apartment, trying to decide what to do. What could she do? Should she call Talia and ask her to come be with her? Certainly, Sabian wouldn't try to take her if she wasn't alone. Would he come and try to take her? And would that happen tonight? She knew she worked herself up into a panic. But it wasn't unwarranted. A demon, or a being from another planet or dimension stalked her. Yes, that sounded silly, even to her. Certainly, if she voiced these thoughts to anyone, she'd be committed.

That was it. She needed to be committed. Nothing could happen to her if she was under observation or medicated. Certainly, they'd heavily medicate her if she told them about Sabian. Her trembling hand took hold of her phone. She dialed nine and then one but paused above the one before dialing the last digit.

A bright burst of white light came from nowhere in the center of the room. It was as though the room split open and bent around it. From within the light, Sabian emerged. He was clothed in black, his eyes were red. He looked more real to her than he had in any of her dreams.

"The time is now. The portal will only remain open for mere seconds. Trust in your heart and in what you know to be true. It is now or never." He reached a hand out to her. "You must come of your own accord."

She found herself moving towards him. She was drawn to him. Before she gave it rational thought, she placed her hand in his. She became surrounded by the brightness and felt herself stretching and flying. The surrounding walls streaked with all the colors of the rainbow. Stars shot by, suns exploded, volcanos erupted and then a peaceful darkness overtook her. She was stationary, laying on her back.

It took a few minutes to force her eyes open. She lay in the middle of the round bed, the soft glow of the blue lights shining up the walls surrounding her. It felt different this time. It felt real.

"Sabian?" She called, sitting up straight.

The lighting in the room adjusted, growing brighter. She saw the doorway to the balcony. Her body was heavy as she stood. It took much effort to walk the dozen steps to the opening. Stepping out, her mind struggled to accept what she saw. There before her was an entire city. Hundreds of spires and domed buildings in beautiful jeweled colors stretched out as far as her eyes could see. There was a light layer of clouds sitting atop the buildings. She was up very high. She wore that strappy, sheer gown that rustled with the light breeze that smelled of citrus.

"My love, you shouldn't be up yet," Sabian spoke from behind her.

She turned to see that he stood in the doorway, his hand reaching towards her. She collapsed into him as he reached her, and he effortlessly lifted her into his arms. He carried her back within the room to where a woman stood. Emma recognized her instantly.

"Mom?" Emma cried. Her mother had not aged a day since she last saw her.

A graceful smile curved over her mother's lips. She'd never seen her mother look so at peace and so happy. "My Emma, my beautiful baby girl. I have dreamed of this day that we would be reunited since I left our world."

Sabian set her to her feet. Her mother swallowed her up in a hug.

"I don't understand," Emma said.

"We are the chosen ones. Mated at conception with one of their kind. Sabian was chosen for you by an all-knowing power, a life force that fuels the universe, just as I was chosen to be with Charon. You will meet him after you have regained your strength and adjusted to the increased gravity of this realm. This is a glorious place. Life is good here."

"There is much for you to learn about this realm," Sabian said. "I will help you navigate it. Have no fear, my love."

"You're not human," she said.

"No, and neither are you," Sabian replied. "The glow of my eyes frightened you but you did not see that yours glowed as well, a soft purple, the essence of your sweet soul."

Emma had so many questions.

"They will wait another day until you have regained your strength," her mother told her as though she could read her mind. And then she embraced Emma before taking her leave.

Sabian embraced her, and she felt pure love and an intense desire radiate from him. He kissed her with soft, firm lips, real lips. She returned his kiss with a hunger that she couldn't control. He untied the bodice of her gown and let it fall to the floor. The lighting grew softer as he laid her to the bed, shedding his own clothes in the process.

"I will not hurt you. You have my word," he whispered across her ear.

The love he made to her was soft and gentle. His hands glided over her body, sending tremors through her from each touch from each caress. Before his legs spread hers, she was wet, throbbing, needing him. He trailed kisses down her neck, over her collarbone, to each waiting breast. His teeth gently bit down on her nipple, sending shockwaves through her. His wet kisses straight down her abdomen sent chills through her and when his lips gave her a lengthy intimate kiss, she exploded in an orgasm so real there was no doubt the others had been in a dream state.

She felt his weight upon her, his rock-hard head against her entry. He gazed into her eyes as he pressed his way in. She trembled with the honesty of the moment, the bareness of her soul exposed to him. At the moment he was fully buried in her, she felt their hearts meld, their souls become one, a fractured being reunited. A realization dawned on her and filled her with peace. For the first time in her life, she was whole. She was home, where she knew she belonged.

Talia ran up the three flights of stairs. She used her copy of Emma's key to open Emma's apartment door. It was three in the afternoon. Emma had missed every meeting on their calendars. She hadn't answered the dozens of phone calls that Talia had placed to her, nor did she answer the many text messages and emails that she'd sent either.

She was afraid what she'd find. Her hand shook as she swung the door open. The apartment was quiet. She left the door open as she stepped in. A quick search confirmed it was empty and there was nobody anywhere in sight. She'd expected to find Emma dead, wrists slit, or hanging from a hook some place. Thank God!

Upon closer inspection, she found Emma's laptop and cell phone on the couch in the living room. Her purse sat on the kitchen table. Her coats hung on the hooks near the door. Nothing seemed to be missing except for Emma.

She dialed nine-one-one. "I need to report a missing person, my best friend, Emma Oliver."

The End

This short story was brought to you by Sisters Romance.

Sisters Romance is the self-publishing imprint of three sisters: RK Cary, Margaret Kay, and Charlie Roberts. All three sisters' books are on Amazon exclusively, read for FREE with Kindle Unlimited or purchase eBooks or paperbacks.

RK Cary writes Science Fiction/Fantasy Erotic Romance with deep plots and in-depth characters. If you enjoyed this short story, give her Destined & Redeemed Trilogy a try. All three books in the trilogy have ranked on Amazon's Best Sellers List for Erotic Science Fiction.

Margaret Kay writes Military Romance. All 16 books published in her Shepherd Security Series (as of March 2025) have ranked on Amazon's Best Sellers List for Action and Adventure Romance, Military Romance, Women's Adventure Fiction, and Police Romance! They are gritty, realistic books with violence, language, and adult sexual situations, not for the faint of heart.

Charlie Roberts writes hot Erotic Contemporary Romantic Fiction and Erotic Romantic Suspense. Saved at Stevens Street is Book #1 in the Stevens Street Series. It is a Romantic Suspense with mystery, and great friendships between believable characters you will fall for. Book #2, Scorched at Stevens Street explores the Dom/Sub relationship entwined in a Romantic Suspense novel. Book #3 is due midsummer 2025. For mature readers only.

Please visit our website to learn more about the Sisters and their books at www.SistersRomance.com

www.ingramcontent.com/pod-product-compliance
Lightning Source LLC
Chambersburg PA
CBHW020648130626
46552CB00003B/1445